A Little Blue Bottle

A Little Blue Bottle

BY JENNIFER GRANT

Illustrated by Gillian Whiting

CHURCH PUBLISHING INCORPORATED

Scripture quotations are taken from the Holy Bible, New Living Transla-
tion, copyright ©1996, 2004, 2015 by Tyndale House Foundation. Used
by permission of Tyndale House Publishers, a Division of Tyndale House
Ministries, Carol Stream, Illinois 60188. All rights reserved.

Church Publishing
19 East 34th Street
New York, NY 10016
www.churchpublishing.org

Cover and interior design: Beth Oberholtzer

A record of this book is available from the Library of Congress.

ISBN-13: 9781640652897 (hardcover)
ISBN-13: 9781640652903 (ebook)

For all who grieve—
may your loneliness be eased
and your hope reawakened.
—J. G.

For my family, thanks for all the love.
—G. W.

Mrs. Wednesday died last Thursday,
or maybe the week before.

All I know is, ever since then,
nothing feels the same anymore.

They loaded
Mrs. Wednesday's furniture onto a truck,
and they drove it far away.

Her daughter picked up Muriel, the ginger cat.

Now Muriel lives some other place.

Muriel used to hide under Mrs. Wednesday's bed
until I'd come and find her.

She purred loud and low
from underneath the bedspread.

"I remember when Mr. Wednesday died,"
my Mama says to me.
"It was before you were even born."

"Muriel was his cat," I tell her.
"Mrs. Wednesday told me that."

"They were married sixty years," Mama says. "She was very sad when he died."

"I feel sad," I tell her.

"She lived next door to me
my whole entire life."

Mama smooths my hair away from my face.

"Did you ever notice that blue bottle
on the windowsill?" she asks.
"Right above her kitchen sink?"

I remember.
There were always three things on that shelf:
a little blue bottle,
African violets with dark purple flowers and fuzzy leaves,
and a picture of Mr. Wednesday in a silver frame.

23

"Not long after Mr. Wednesday died,
she and I were having a cup of tea," Mama says.

"She had just bought that little blue bottle, and she took it out and showed it to me."

"There's a verse in the Bible
that says that God knows when we cry
and saves every one of our tears
in a bottle," Mama says.

"Sometimes, over the years, she told me that
when she was missing Mr. Wednesday
or just felt lonely
or was having a hard day,
she held that little blue bottle and
imagined God was collecting her tears in it,"
Mama says.

I try to imagine my tears falling into
a blue bottle and God saving them,
every single one.

And I wonder if it could be true.

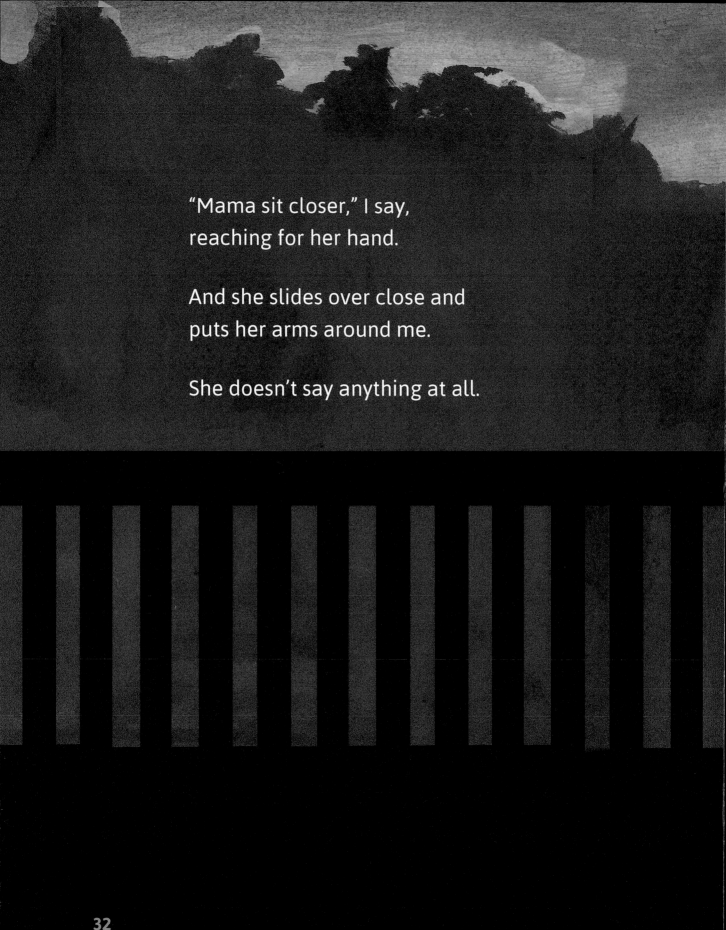

"Mama sit closer," I say,
reaching for her hand.

And she slides over close and
puts her arms around me.

She doesn't say anything at all.

Mrs. Wednesday died last Thursday,
or maybe the week before.

All I know is ever since then,
nothing feels the
same anymore.

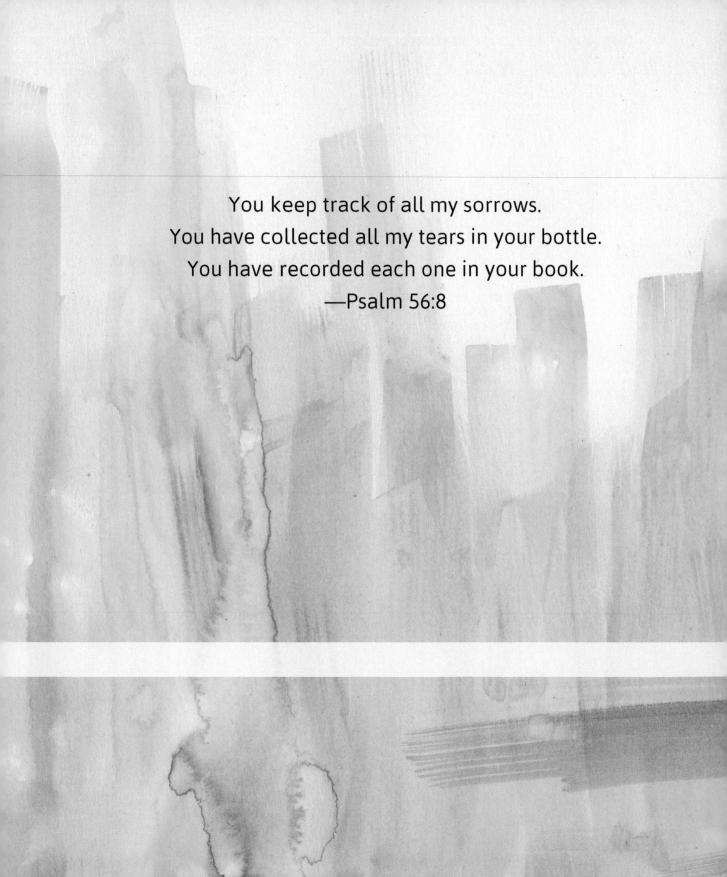

You keep track of all my sorrows.
You have collected all my tears in your bottle.
You have recorded each one in your book.
—Psalm 56:8

Best Practices for When a Child Is Grieving

- Be honest, and use simple language when discussing death.

- Avoid euphemisms such as "lost," "departed," "passed," or "asleep," as children can take such terms literally.

- Consider the child's developmental stage when discussing death. Younger children often think death is reversible; some think it's contagious.

- Share your own beliefs and rituals regarding death with children, allowing them to be involved, when appropriate. Children may benefit from laying flowers at a gravesite, planting a tree in memory of a deceased person, looking through pictures, and talking about special times with the person who has died.

- Let the child feel sad, angry, or confused—or whatever emotions surface. Understand that, for younger children, developmental and behavioral regressions may occur. Children, as is true for adults, might have trouble sleeping when they are grieving.

- Communicate security by being present, listening, and expressing affection to your child. In the aftermath of a loved one's death, children will often fear that they will not be taken care of—assure them that they will be cared for either by you or another trusted person. Consider sharing with children that you have made a loving plan for their care, should anything happen to you.

- It is okay to show your own grief, letting children see how sadness is experienced and processed. If your grief becomes overwhelming to you, seek adult support to help you through this difficult time.

- Understand that grief will look different in children than in adults; a child may be sad one moment and then seem carefree the next.

For more resources, visit The Dougy Center (The National Center for Grieving Children and Families) at www.dougy.org.

Jennifer Grant is the author of several books for adults, including the adoption memoir, *Love You More*. Her work for children includes the award-winning picture book *Maybe God Is Like That Too*. The mother of four and a lifelong Episcopalian, she lives in the Chicago area with her husband and rescue dog, Scarlett. Connect with her online at jennifergrant.com.

Gillian Whiting studied Illustration at Syracuse University. Though she has been creating all art in all forms for as long as she can remember, this is her first published work. She is already looking forward to her next project, and a future filled with art and creativity!